LAST CALL FROM
SECTOR 9G

LAST CALL FROM SECTOR 9G

by Leigh Brackett

Out there in the green star system; far beyond the confining grip of the Federation, moved the feared Bitter Star, for a thousand frigid years the dark and sinister manipulator of war-weary planets.

CHAPTER I.

Martie said monotonously, "There is someone at the door Sir, shall I answer? There is someone at the door Sir, shall I?"

Durham grunted. What he wanted to say was go away and let me alone. But he would only grunt, and Artie kept repeating the stupid question. Artie was a cheap off-brand make and bought used and he lacked some cogs. Any first class servall would have seen that the master had passed out in his chair and was in no condition to receive guests. But Artie did not, and presently Durham got one eye open and then he began to hear the persistent knocking, the annunciator being naturally out of order. And he said quite clearly.

"If it's a creditor, I'm not in."

"Shall I answer?"

Durham made a series of noises. Artie took them for an affirmative and trundled off. Durham put his face in his hands and struggled with the pangs of returning consciousness, He could hear a mutter of voices in the hall. He thought suddenly that he recognized them, and he sprang, or rather stumbled up in alarm, hastily combing his hair with his fingers and trying to pull the wrinkles out of his tunic. Through a thick haze he saw the bottle on the table, and he picked it up and hid it under a chair, ashamed not of its emptiness but of its label. A gentleman should not be drunk on stuff like that.

Paulsen and Burke came in.

Durham stood stiffly beside the table, hanging on. He looked at the two men. "Well," he said. "It's been quite a long time." He turned to Artie. "The gentlemen are leaving."

Burke stepped quickly behind the servall and pushed the main toggle to OFF, Artie stopped, with a sound ridiculously like a tired sigh. Paulsen went past him and locked the door. Then both of them turned in to face Durham.

Durham scowled. "What the devil do you think you're doing?"

Burke and Paulsen glanced at each other as though resolve had carried them this far but had now run out, leaving them irresolute in the face of some distasteful task. Both men wore black dominos, with the cowls thrown back.

"Were you afraid you'd be recognized coming here?" Durham said. A small pulse of fright began to beat in him, and this was idiotic. It made him angry. "What do you want?"

Paulsen said in a reluctant voice, not looking at him, "I don't want anything Durham, believe me." Durham had once been engaged to Paulsen's sister, a thing both of them preferred not to ren but couldn't quite forget. He went on, "We were sent here."

Durham tried to think who might sent them. Certainly not any of the girls; certainly not any one of the people he owed money to. Two members of the Terran World Embassy corps, even young and still obscure members in the lower echelons, were above either of those missions.

"Who sent you?"

Burke said, "Hawtree."

"No," said Durham. "Oh no, you got the name wrong. Hawtree wouldn't send for me if I was the last man in the galaxy. Hawtree, indeed."

"Hawtree," said Paulsen. He drew a deep breath and threw aside his domino. "Come on, Burke."

Burke took off his domino. They came on together.

Durham drew back. His shoulders dropped and his fists came up. "Look out," he said. "What you going to do? Look out!"

"All right," said Burke, and they both jumped together and caught his arms, not because Durham was so big or so powerful that he frightened them, but because they disliked the idea of brawling with a drunken man. Paulsen said,

"Hawtree wants you tonight, and he wants you sober, and that, damn it, is the way he's going to get you."

*

An hour and seven minutes later Durham sat beside Paulsen in a 'copter with no insigne and watched the roof of his apartment tower fall away beneath him.

Burke had stayed behind, and Durham wore the Irishman's domino with the cowl up over his head. Under the domino was his good suit, the one he had not sent to the pawnbroker because he could not, as yet, quite endure being without one good suit. He was scrubbed and shaved and perfectly sober. Outside he did not look too bad. Inside he was a shamble.

The 'copter fitted itself into a north-south lane. Paulsen, muffled in his cowl, sat silent. Durham felt a similar reluctance to speak. He looked out over The Hub and tried to keep from thinking. Don't run to meet it, don't get your hopes up. Whatever it is, let it happen, quietly.

The city was beautiful. Its official name was Galactic Center, but it was called The Hub because that is what it was, the hub and focus of a galaxy. It was the biggest city in the Milky Way. It covered almost the entire land area of the third planet of a Type G star that someone

7

with a sense of humor had christened Pax. The planet was chosen originally because it was centrally located and had no inhabitants, and because it was within the limits of tolerance for the humanoid races. The others mostly needed special accommodations anyway.

And so from a sweet green any world with nothing on it but trees and grass and a few mild-natured animals The Hub had grown to have a population of something like ten billion people, spread horizontally and stacked up vertically and dug in underneath, and every one of them was engaged in some governmental function, or in espionage, or in both. Intrigue was as much a part of life in The Hub as corpuscles are a part of blood. The Hub boasted that it the only inhabited world in space where no single grain of wheat or saddle of mutton was grown, where nothing was manufactured, and nobody worked at a manual job.

Durham loved it passionately.

Both moons were in the sky now. One was small and low, like a white pearl hung

just out of reach. The other was enormous. It had an atmosphere, and it served as warehouse and supply base for the planet city, handling the billions of tons of shipping that kept it going. The two of them made a glorious spectacle, but Durham did not bother to see them. The vast glow of the city paled them, made them unimportant. He was remembering how he had seen it when he was fresh from Earth, for the first time the supreme capital, beside which the world capitals were only toy cities, the heart and center of the galaxy where the decisions were made, and the great men came and went. He was remembering how he had felt how he had been so sure of the future that he never gave it a second thought.

But something happened.

What?

8

Liquor, they said, and the accident.

No, not liquor, the hell with them. I could always carry my drinks.

The accident. Well, what of it? Didn't other people have accidents? And anyway, nobody really got hurt out of it. He didn't, and the girl didn't, what if she wasn't his fiancée? And the confidential file he had in the 'copter hadn't fallen into anybody's hands. So, there wasn't anything to that.

No. Not liquor and not the accident, no matter what they said. It was Hawtree, and a personal grudge because he, Durham, had had Hawtree's daughter out with him in the 'copter that night. And so what? He was only engaged to Willa Paulsen, not married to her, and anyway Susan Hawtree knew what she was doing. She knew darn well.

Hawtree, a grudge, and a little bad luck. That's what happened. And that's all.

The 'copter swerved and dropped onto a private landing stage attached to a penthouse. Durham knew it well, though he hadn't seen it for over a year. He got out, aware of palpitations and a gone feeling in the knees. He needed a drink, but he knew that he would have to go inside first, and he forced himself to stand up and walk beside Paulsen as though nothing had ever happened. The head high, the face proud and calm, just a touch of bitterness but not too much.

Hawtree was alone in the living room. He glanced at Durham as he came in through the long glass doors. There was a servall standing in the corner and Hawtree said to it, "A drink for the gentleman, straight and stiff."

A small anger stirred in Durham Hawtree might at least have given him the choice. He said sharply, "No thanks."

Hawtree said, "Don't be a fool." He looked tired, but then he always had. Tired and keyed up, full of the drive and the brittle excitement of one who has juried peoples and nations, expressed as black marks on sheets of varicolored paper for so long that it has become a habit as necessary and destructive as hashish. To Paulsen he said, "I'll ring when I need you "

Paulsen went out. The servall placed the drink in Durham's hand. He did not refuse it.

"Sit down," said Hawtree, and Durham sat, Hawtree dismissed the servall. Durham drank part of his drink and felt better. Well, he said, "I'm listening".

"You were a great disappointment to me, Durham."

"What am I supposed to say to that?"

"Nothing. Go ahead, finish your drink, I want to talk to a man, not a zombie."

Durham finished it angrily. "If you brought me all the way here to shake your finger at me, I'm going home again." That was what he said aloud. Inside, he wanted to get down and embrace Hawtree's knees and beg him for another chance.

"I brought you here," said Hawtree, "to offer you a job. If you do it, it might mean that certain doors could be opened for you again.

Durham sat perfectly still. For a moment he did not trust himself to speak. Then he said, "I'll take it."

Certain doors. That's what I've waited for, living like a bum, dodging creditors, hocking my shoes, waiting for those doors to open again.

*

He tried not to show how he felt, sitting stiffly at ease in the chair, but a red flush began to burn in his cheeks and his hands moved. About time. About time, damn you, Hawtree, that you remembered me.

Damn you, oh damn you for making me sweat so long!

10

Hawtree said, "Did you ever hear of Nanta Dik?"

"No. What is it?"

"A planet. It belongs to a green star system, chart designation KL421, Sub-sector 9G, Sector 80, Quadrant 7. It's a very isolated system, the only inhabited one in 9G, as a matter of fact. 9G is a Terran quota sector, and since Nanta Dik is humanoid, it's become headquarters for our nationals who are engaged in business in that sub-sector."

Durham nodded. Unassimilated territory lying outside the Federation was divided among Federation members, allowing them to engage in trade only in their allotted sectors and subject to local law and license. This eliminated competitive friction between Federation worlds, threw open new areas to development, and eventually, usually under the sponsorship of the federated world, brought the quota sectors into the vast family of suns that had already spread over more than half the galaxy. There were abuses now and again, but on the w I as a system, it worked pretty well.

"I take it that Nanta Dik is where I'm going."

"Yes. Now listen. First thing in the morning, go and book a third-class passage to Earth on the Sylvania Merchant, leaving on the day following. Let your friends know you're going home. They won't be surprised."

"Don't rub it in."

"Sorry. When you reach the spaceport walk across the main rotunda near the newsstand. Drop your ticket and your passport, folded together, go on to the newsstand and wait. They will be returned to you by a uniformed attendant, only your passport will be in a different name and your ticket will now be on a freighter outbound for Nanta Dik. You will then embark at once. Is that all clear?"

11

"Everything but the reason."

"I'll come to that. How good is your memory?"

"As good as it ever was."

"All right. When you reach Nanta Dik a man will meet you as you leave the ship. He will ask if you are the ornithologist. You will say yes. Then pay close attention to this you will say, the darkbirds will soon fly. Got that?"

"The darkbirds will soon fly. Simple enough. What does it mean?"

"9G is a rich sector, isolated, improperly policed, underpopulated. There has been a certain amount of trouble, poaching, claim jumping, outright piracy. The 'darkbirds' are a couple of suspected ships. We want to set a trap for them, and you know how things are on The Hub. If a man buys a pair of socks, the news is all across the galaxy in a week. That's the reason for all the secrecy."

"Is that all?"

"No." Hawtree got up, turning his I on Durham. He said harshly, "Listen Lloyd." It was the first time he had used Durham's Christian name. "This is an important job. It may not seem like one, but it is. Do it. There's somebody else who let you to have another chance."

Durham did not say anything. He waited for Hawtree to turn around and face him and say the name. But he didn't, and finally Durham said,

"Susan?"

"I don't know what she sees in you," said Hawtree, and pushed a button. Paulsen came in. Hawtree jerked a thumb at Durham. "Take him back. And tell Burke to give him the money."

Durham went out and got into the 'copter. He felt dizzy, and this time it was not from drinks or the lack of them. He sat, and Paulsen took the 'copter off.

12

Hawtree watched it from inside the glass doors until it was out of sight above the roof. And another man came from behind a door that led into Hawtree's private study and watched it with him.

"Are you sure about him?" asked the man.

"I know him," Hawtree said. "He's a slob."

"But are you sure?"

"Don't worry, Morrison," Hawtree said. "I know him. He'll talk. Bet you a hundred he never even makes the spaceport."

"Blessed are the fools," said Morrison, "for they shall inherit nothing."

CHAPTER II.

Baya sat on the bed and watched him pack. She was from one of the worlds of Mintaka, and as humanoid as they came, not very tall but very well shaped, and colored one beautiful shade of old bronze from the crown of her head to the soles of her feet, except for her mouth, which was a vivid red.

"It seems funny," she said, "to think of you not being here tomorrow."

"Will you die of missing me?""

"Probably, for a day or two. I was comfortable. I hate upheavals."

Durham reached across her for his small stack of underwear. She was wearing the yellow silk thing that made her skin glow-by contrast. He saw that it was dubiously clean about the neck, and when he paused to kiss her, he noticed the tiny lines around her mouth and eyes, the indefinable look of wear and hardness that was more destructive to beauty than the mere passing of years. Yesterday they had been two of a kind, part of the vast backwash left behind by other people's successes. Today he was far above her. And he was glad.

"The least you could do," she said, "would be to make this a really big evening. But I suppose you couldn't run to that."

"I've got money." Burke had given him some, but that was for expenses and he would neither mention it nor touch it. "Artie brought a pretty good price, so did the furniture." There was nothing left in the apartment but the bed, and even that was sold. He had bought back a few of his better belongings, and he still had a wad of credits. He felt good. He felt joyous and expansive. He felt like a man again. He poured two drinks and handed one to Baya.

"All right," he said, "here's to a big last evening. The biggest."

LAST CALL FROM SECTOR 9G

They had cocktails in a bar called The Moonraker because it was the highest point in that hemisphere of the city. It was the hour between sunset and moonrise, when the towers stood sharply defined against a sky of incredible dark blueness, with the brighter stars pricked out in it, and the dim canyons at the feet of the towers were lost in the new night, spectral, soft and lovely. And the night deepened, and the lights came on.

They wandered for a while among the high flung walkways that spanned the upper levels of the towers so that people need not spend half their lives in elevators. They skirted the vast green concourse from which the halls of government rose up white and unadorned and splendid. They only skirted one corner of it, because this galactic Capitol Hill ran for miles, dominating the whole official complex, and one enormous building of it was fitted up so that the non-humanoid Members of Universal Parliament could "attend" the sessions in comfort, never leaving their especially pressurized and congenially poisonous suites. Between humanoid and non-humanoid there were many scientific gradations of form. But for governmental purposes it boiled down simply to oxygen-breather or non-oxygen-breather.

"Human or not," said Durham, standing on an upper span, with the good liquor burning bright inside him, "human or not, they're only men like me. What they've done, I can do."

"This is dull," said Baya.

"Dull," said Durham. He shook his head in wonderment, staring at her. She was beautiful. Tonight, she wore white, and her hair curled softly on her neck, and her mouth was languorous, and her eyes, her eyes were hard. They were always hard, always making a liar out of that pliant, generous mouth. "Doll, he said. "No wonder you never got anywhere."

16

LEIGH BRACKETT

She flared up at that and said a few things about him. He knew they were no longer true, so he could afford to be amused by them. He smiled and said,

"Let's not quarrel, Baya. This is goodbye, remember. Come on, we'll have a drink at the Miran."

They floated down on the bright spider web levels of the walkways, drifting east, stopping at the Miran and then going on to another drinking place, and then to another. The walks were thronged with other people, people from hundreds of stars, thousands of worlds. People of an infinite variety of sizes, shapes and colors, dressed in every imaginable and unimaginable fashion. Ambassadors, MP's, wives and mist couriers, calculator jockeys, topologists and graph men, office girls, hairdressers, janitors, pimps, you-name-it. Durham saw them through a golden haze, and loved them, because they were the city and he was a part of them again.

He was out of the backwash of not-being. Hawtree had had to give in, and this footling errand to some dust speck nobody ever heard of was simply a necessary device to save his own face. All right, Hawtree, fine. We will go along with the gag. And you may inform the haughty Miss Hawtree, who can, believe us, be also the naughty Miss Hawtree, that we don't know if we want her back or not. We'll see.

"—take me with you," Baya was saying. Durham shook his head. "Lone trip, honey. Can't possibly."

"Are you ashamed of me, Lloyd? That's it, you're ashamed to take me to Earth."

"No. No. Now, Baya.'"

He looked at her. His vision was a bit blurred by now, he could see just enough background to wonder how the devil they'd got to this closed-in-looking drinking place. But Baya's face was clear enough. She was crying.

"Now, Baya, honey, it's not that, it's not that at all."

"Then why can't I go with you to Earth?"

"Because, listen Baya, can you keep a secret?" He laughed, and his own laughter sounded blurred too. "Promise?"

"Promise."

"I..."

*

Dead stop. The words rattled on his tongue but remained unspoken. Why? Was it because of Baya's eyes, that wept tears but had no sorrow in them? He could see them quite clearly, and they were not sorrowful at all, but avid.

"I promised, Lloyd. You can tell me." There was a table under his hands, with an exotically patterned cloth on it. He had no memory of having sat down at it. There was a wall of plastic cement covered with a crude mural in bright primaries. There was a low, vaulted ceiling, also painted. There were no windows.

"How did we get here?" Durham asked stupidly. "It's underground."

"It's just a place," Baya said impatiently. And then she said sharply, "What's the matter with you?"

Blood and fumes hammered together in his bulging temples, and his back felt cold. "Where's the men's room, Baya?"

Her mouth set in anger and disgust. She called, "Varnik!"

A tall powerful man with a very long neck and skin the color of a ripe plum came up to the table. He wore an apron.

Baya said, "Better take him there, Varnik."

The plum colored man took him and ran him to a door and put him through it. From there a servall took over. It was very efficient.

"Are you through, sir?"

"God, no. Not nearly."

One more word and you would have been through. Forever. Drunken blabbermouth Durham, smart aleck Durham, would-be big shot Durham, ready to babble out his secret and blow his last chance of a comeback. But why did Baya have to be so insistently curious?

Why, indeed?

He began to feel both sick and scared.

After a time, he made it to the row of basins and splashed cold water on his face and head. There was a mirror above the basin. He looked into it. "Hello, bum," he said.

Face it, Durham. You're a drunken bum. You are exactly what Willa Paulsen said you were, what Susan Hawtree said you were, what they all said you were. You get a second chance, and you go right out and get drunk and blow it Or, almost. Another minute and you'd have blabbed everything you know to Baya.

Baya, who cried because he wouldn't tell her; who had brought him to this rathole. He took a clearer look at it when he went shakily out of the men's room. The place almost empty, and it had a close, smothery feeling. Durham had never liked these underground streets, this vaguely un-demi-world that wound itself around the foundations of the city. It was considered smart to go slumming here, but this place was somehow wrong.

There were a man and woman at a table across the room, a young, pale green couple who pretended too carefully not to see him. There was Varnik, the plum colored proprietor, at a tall desk beside the main door. And there was Baya at their table.

She handed him a glass when he came over. "Feel better? I ordered you a sedative." Without sitting down, he put the glass to his lips. It did not taste like any sedative he could remember, and he thought he had tried them all.

"I don't want it."

LAST CALL FROM SECTOR 9G

"Don't be a fool, Lloyd. Take it." Her eyes were cold now, and he was suddenly quite sure why he had been brought here.

Durham said softly, "Good night, tramp. God night and good-bye." He ran around the table and made a rush for the entrance.

Varnik stepped from the tall desk to bar his way, holding out a piece of paper. "Sir," he said. "Your check."

Durham heard three chairs scrape behind him. He did not pause. He bent and drove the point of his shoulder as hard as he could at a spot just above Varnik's wide belt. Varnik let go a gasping sigh and wheeled away. Durham went out the door.

The underground street was brightly lighted. It ran straight to right and left, under a low roof, and disappeared on either hand around a right-angle turn. Durham went to the left for no particular reason. There were people on the street. He dodged among them, running. They stopped and stared at him, and there was an echo of other feet behind him, also running. He sped around the corner, and it occurred to him that he was completely lost, that he did not even know what part of the city lay above him, or how far. There were different levels to this under-city, following down the foundations, the conduits and tubes and sewers and pumping stations. For the first time he began to feel genuinely afraid.

The street ran straight ahead until it ended against a buttressed foundation wall. There were doors and windows on either side of it. People lived here. There were joints, some fancy-exotic for the carriage trade, others just joints. A couple of smaller streets opened off it, darker and more winding. Durham plunged into one, pausing briefly to look back. Fleeting like deer around the corner were the young pale green couple who had sat at the other table in Varnik's. There was something about the purposeful way they ran that sent a quiver of pure terror through Durham's insides.

He ran again, as hard as he could, wondering who the devil they were and what they wanted with him.

What did anyone want with him, and the small bit of a secret he carried?

THE narrow street wound and twined. Clearly echoing along the vault of the roof he could hear footsteps. One. Two. Coming fast. He saw an opening no wider than a crack in the wall. He turned into it. It was quite dark in there and he knew he could not go much farther, and that fact added to his burden of shame. There had been a time when this much of a sprint would hardly have breathed him. He tottered on, looking for a place to hide in, and there wasn't any, and his heart banged and floundered against his ribs, and the muscles of his thighs were like wet strings.

There was a square opening with blank walls all around it and a great big manhole cover in the middle. There was the way he had come in, and there was another narrow way he might have come out, but Varnik was coming through it, running a little crooked and breathing hard. He stopped when he saw Durham. Baya, panting up behind, almost ran into him. Varnik grunted and sprang.

With feeble fierceness, Durham resisted. It got him nowhere. The plum colored man struck him several times out of pure pique, cursing Durham for making trouble, for bruising his gut, for making him run like this. Baya stood by and watched.

"Will you behave now?" Varnik demanded. He whacked Durham again, and Durham glared at him out of dazed eyes and felt the world tilt and slide away from him.

Suddenly there were new voices, footsteps, confusion. He fell, what seemed a long way but was really only to his hands and knees.

The young couple had come into the square space. They were small lithe people, muscled like ocelots, and their skin color was a pale

21

green, very pretty, and characteristic of several different races, but no good for identification here. The girl's tunic had slipped aside over the breast, and the skin there was a clear gold, like new country butter. They both had guns in their strong little fists, and they were speaking over Durham to Varnik and Baya.

"We will question this man alone."

"Oh, no," said Varnik angrily. "You don't get away with that."

Baya bent over Durham. "Come on, lover," she said. "Get up." Her voice was cooing. To the strangers she said, "That wasn't our deal at all."

"You failed," said the girl with the two-colored skin, and she fired a beam with frightening accuracy, exactly between them.

A piece of the wall behind them fused and flared. Varnik's eyes came wide open.

"Well," he said. "Well, if that's the way you feel about it."

He turned. Baya hesitated, and the muzzle of the gun began to move her way. She snarled something in her own language and decided to go after Varnik.

Durham got his hands and feet bunched under him. He didn't know what he was going to do, but he knew that once he was left alone with the two small fleet strangers he would eventually talk, and after that it would not matter much what happened to him.

He said to them, hopefully, "You have the wrong man. I don't know"

There were the five of them in the small space. There were the two couples facing each other, and Durham on his knees between them. And then there was something else.

There was a spiky shadow, perfectly black, of undetermined size and nameless shape, except that it was spiky.

Baya did not quite scream. She pressed against Varnik, and they both recoiled into the alley mouth. The young couple paled under their greenness, and they, too, drew back. Durham crouched on the ground.

The shadow bounded and rolled and leaped through the air and hung cloudlike over Durham's head. Suddenly it shrieked out, in a high, toneless voice like that of a deaf child, a clatter of gibberish in which one syllable stood clear, repeated several times.

"Jubb!" said the shadow. "Jubb! Jubb! Jubb!"

CHAPTER III.

Jubb. It might have been a name, a curse, or a battle cry. Whatever it was, the young couple did not like it. Their faces twisted into slim masks of hate. They raised their guns at the shadow, and the shadow laughed. Abruptly it bunched up small and shot at them.

Durham heard them yell, in pain or fright or both, and he heard their running feet, but he did not see what happened to them. He was going away himself, down the narrow alley that Varnik and Baya were no longer interested in blocking. When he reached the end of the alley, he came out onto a well-lighted street with lots of people on it, but he still did not feel safe.

Varnik and Baya were not far away. Baya was leaning against a wall with her mouth wide open. She was not used to running. Varnik was standing beside her looking sulky. He scowled at Durham when he came out of the alley. Durham stopped, bracing himself and ready to yell for help. But Varnik shook his head "Nyuh!" he said.

Baya panted. "What's the matter, you afraid?"

"Yes," said Varnik. "Those two little green ones, they are not playing for fun. And that black one..." He quivered all over. "I'm afraid. I see you again, Baya."

He went away. Baya was close onto tears, partly from her own fright, partly from sheer fury and frustration. But she did not.

She turned and looked at Durham. "What got into you?" she said. "It was all set, and then you had to louse it up." She cursed him. "It's just like you, Lloyd, to cost me a nice chunk of money."

"Who are those people, Baya?"

"They didn't tell me. I didn't ask."

"Total strangers, eh?"

"Turned up this afternoon at my apartment. I should think you could tell. They're not the type I run with."

25

"No." He frowned, still breathing hard and wiping sweat from his face. "How did they know about us?"

She shrugged, and said maliciously, "Somebody must have told them. Well, so long, Lloyd. I wish you all the luck you deserve."

She walked off slowly, patting her hair into place, straightening the line of her white dress. She did not look back. Durham watched her for a second. Then he began to walk fast as he could in the opposite direction, keeping in the brightest lights. After a bit he found a stair walk. He rode up on it through two levels, and all the while the roots of his hair were prickling, and he was darting nervous glances over his shoulder and into the air over his head.

Jubb. Jubb. Jubb.

He envied Varnik who could go away and forget the whole thing.

It was still night when he reached the surface. The shadow did not seem to have followed him, but how could you tell? Even a city as brilliantly lighted as The Hub always has shadowy corners by night. He kept listening for that high, flat, hooting voice. It did not speak to him, and he hailed a sky cab, appalled by how little time he had left to catch the pre-dawn ferry.

He made it with no minutes to spare. He found a place on the dark side and settled himself for the four-hour run, and then everything caught up to him at once and he began to shake. He sat there in the grip of a violent reaction, living over again Hawtree's instructions and the evening with Baya and the nightmare run through the underground streets, and the coming of the shadow. The dark birds will soon fly. Was that enough for people to kill for? It might be if they had an interest in those ships, but the young couple did not look the type. And the shadow?

He shivered and looked out the port. The long thin shadow of the ship extended itself indefinitely into space, but all around it there was

26

light, and the curve of the planet below was a blaze of gold. Down there was Hawtree and a big part of his life. Above and ahead was the huge cool face of the moon, and that was the future, all unexplored. Durham clenched his cold hands together between his knees and thought, I've got to do this, stay sober and do it, a little for Hawtree but mostly for myself. A man can't look at himself twice the way I did tonight. Once is all he can stand. And once ought to be enough.

The brightness blurred and swam. Presently he slept, and his dreams were thronged shadows hooting "Jubb! Jubb! Jubb!"

Four hours later Durham walked across the vast main rotunda of the lunar spaceport, dropping his little bundle of passport and ticket as casually as he could. He continued on to the newsstand and made a pretense of looking over the half credit micro books, waiting.

While he waited, he wondered. He wondered how the young couple had known about Baya. He wondered what the shadow md where it came from, and why it had defended him from the young couple, and what was the meaning of the rather ridiculous word "Jubb." He wondered if he wasn't crazy not to pick up his ticket to Earth and use it.

He wanted a drink very badly.

A uniformed attendant came and said "I think you dropped this, sir."

He held out a passport with a ticket folded in it. Durham examined them, put them in his pocket, and tipped the attendant, who went away. Durham bought three micro books and moved on. He could not see anybody watching him, and he told himself it was only nerves that made the skin creep on his back as though eyes were boring into it.

The switch had been made all right on his papers. His name was now John Mills Watson and he had a passage to Nanta Dik aboard the freighter Margaretta K. He still wanted a drink. He was determined that he would not go and get it, and he headed grimly for a stair walk that led down to the port cab system. He had almost stepped onto it, and then from the loudspeakers all over the huge rotunda a voice boomed out, saying, "Mr. Lloyd Durham, please come to the Information Desk."

Durham flinched as though somebody had struck him. He thought, Hawtree's sent word to recall me. Perhaps it was a trap.

*

He approached the desk cautiously, while his name continued to blare forth from the loudspeakers. Somebody was standing there. A woman, with her back to him. He had not seen that back for over a year, not since the night of the accident, but he had not forgotten it.

"Hello, Susan," he said.

She turned around, and he added bitterly, "He needn't have sent you." He was convinced now that she had come to call him back.

She seemed surprised. "Who?"

"Your father."

"Dad? Good heavens, Lloyd, you don't suppose he knows I'm here!" She was tall, as he remembered her, and handsome, and beautifully dressed, and very self-assured. She smiled, one of those brittle things with no humor in it, and then she asked, "How long have you before take-off?"

Durham said slowly, "Time enough."

"We can't talk here."

"No. Come on, I'll buy you a drink."

They walked in silence to the crowded, noisy spaceport bar. They found a place and sat down. Durham ordered. Susan Hawtree sat opening and closing her handbag as though the operation was of the most absorbing interest.

He asked, "Why did you come here?" "It seemed as though somebody ought to say good-bye."

"Who told you I was leaving?"

"I have a friend in the travel office. She tells me if anybody I know books passage home."

"Convenient."

"Yes."

The drinks came. There was a clatter of voices, speaking in a thousand tongues, laughing, crying, saying hello and good-bye and till we meet again. Susan turned her glass round and round in her fingers, and Durham watched her.

"I'm sorry, Lloyd. Sorry everything could not have turned out better."

"Yes. So am I."

"I hope you'll have better luck at home."

"Thanks."

Another silence in which Durham tried hard to figure her angle.

He said, "I heard you tried to talk your father into giving me another chance. Thanks for that."

She stared at him blankly and shook her head. "You know how Dad feels about you. I've never dared mention your name." A cold feeling settled in the pit of Durham's stomach. There's somebody else, Lloyd, who wanted you to have another chance. Fatherly intuition?

Or a big fat lie?

Let's face it, Durham, why would Hawtree send you on a mission to the dog pound? There are ten billion people on The Hub. He could have found somebody else.

LAST CALL FROM SECTOR 9G

The whole business smells. It reeks. But wait. Suppose he sent Susan here to test me; to see if I'd talk? Not too believable, but a pleasanter belief than the alternative. Let's see.

"Susan. Look, I can say this now because I'm going home and that's the end of it. We won't see each other anymore. I should never have got engaged to Willa; I didn't love her. It was you all the time."

He caught the quick glint of tears in her eyes and was appalled. Tears for him? From Susan Hawtree?

That's why I went with you that night," she whispered. "I thought I could take you from her. I thought I could make you be what you ought to be, damn you, Lloyd, I should never have come here!"

She jumped up and walked rapidly a from the table. He followed her, with his I his eyes and his mouth both wide open and something very strange happening inside him.

One thing sure. She was no plant.

"Susan."

"Don't you have to get aboard or something?"

"Yes, but Susan, ride down with me I want to talk to you."

"There's nothing to talk about. But she went to the stair walk with him, and rode down, her face turn, her head held so high she seemed to tower over him.

"Susan," he said. "Do you think, could you give me"

"No, that's not the gambit."

"But what do you say, Susan, I'm a changed man. Susan, wait for me?"

The stair walk slid them gently off onto a very long platform. There was a crowd on it, sorting itself into the endless lines of purple monorail taxis that moved along both sides.

"Susan."

"Good-bye, Lloyd."

"No, wait a minute. Please I don't know quite how."

Suddenly they were not alone. A young couple had joined them. The color of their skin had changed from pale green to a n burnt orange, and their clothing was different, but Durham recognized them without difficulty. A hard object prodded him in the side, and the young man, smiling, said to him, "Get into that cab."

The woman, also smiling, said to Susan Hawtree, "Don't scream. Keep perfectly quiet."

Susan's face went white. She looked at Durham, and Durham said to the young man, "Let her go, she has nothing to do with this."

"Get in the cab." said the young man.

"Both of you."

"I think," said Susan, "we'd better do it."

They got in. The doors closed automatically behind them. The young man, with his free hand, took out a ticket and laid it in the scanner slot, with the code number of the ship's docking area uppermost. The taxi clicked, hummed, and took off smoothly.

Durham saw the ticket as the young man removed it from the scanner. It was a passage to Nanta Dik aboard the freighter Margaretta K.

CHAPTER IV.

The monorails came out onto the surface in bunches like very massive cables and then began to branch out, the separate "wires" of the cables eventually spreading into a network that covered the entire moon. The taxi picked up speed, clicking over points as it swerved and swung, feeling its way onto the one clear track that led where its scanner had told it to go. Durham was aware obliquely of other monorail taxis in uncountable numbers going like the devil in all directions, and of other types of machines moving below on the surface, and of mobile cranes that walked like buildings, and of an horizon filled with the upthrust noses of great ships like the towers of some fantastic city. Beside him Susan Hawtree sat, rigid and quivering, and before him on the opposite seat were the two young people with the guns.

Durham said, in a voice thick with anger and fright, "Why did you have to drag her into it?"

The man shrugged. "She is perhaps part of the conspiracy. In any case, she would have made an alarm."

"What do you mean, conspiracy? I'm going home to Earth. She came to say goodbye." Durham leaned forward. "You're the same two bastards from last night. What do you..."

"Please," said the man, contemptuously. He gestured with the gun. "You will both sit still with your hands behind your heads. So. Wanbecq-ai will search you. If either one should attempt to interfere, the other will suffer for it."

The wiry young woman did her work swiftly and efficiently. "No weapons," she said. "Hai! Wanbecq, look here!" She began to gabble in a strange tongue, pointing to Durham's passport and ticket, and then to Susan's ID card. Wanbecq's narrow eyes narrowed still further.

"So," he said to Durham. "Your name has changed since yesterday, Mr. Watson. And for one who returns to Sol III, you choose a long way around."

Susan stared hard at Durham. "What's he talking about?"

"Never mind. Listen, you, Wanbecq, is that your name? Miss Hawtree has nothing to do with any of this. Her father..."

"Is a part of the embassy which sent you out," said Wanbecq, flicking Susan's ID card with his finger. "Do not expect me to believe foolishness, Mr. Watson-Durham." He spoke rapidly to Wanbecq-ai. She nodded, and they both turned to Susan.

"Obviously you were sent with instructions for Mr. Durham, Will you tell us now what they were?"

Susan's face was such a blank of amazement that Durham would have laughed if the situation had not been so extremely unfunny.

"Nobody sent me with anything. Nobody even knows I came. Lloyd, are these people crazy? Are you crazy? What's going on here?"

He said, "I'm not sure myself. But I think there are only two possibilities. One, your father is a scoundrel. Two, he's a fool being used by scoundrels. Take your pick. In either case, I'm the goat."

Her white cheeks turned absolutely crimson. She tried twice to say something to Durham. Then she turned and said to the Wanbecqs, "I've had enough of this. Let me out."

They merely glanced at her and went on talking.

"You might as well relax," said Durham to her, in colloquial English, hoping the Wanbecqs could not understand it. "I'm sorry you got into this, and I'll try to get you out, but don't do anything silly."

She called him a name she had never learned in the Embassy drawing rooms. There was a manual switch recessed in the body of the taxi, high up and sealed in with a special plastic. It said

EMERGENCY on it. Susan took off her shoe and swung. The plastic shattered. Susan dropped the shoe and grabbed for the switch. Wanbecq yelled. Wanbecq-ai leaped headlong for in and bore her back onto the seat. She was using her gun flatwise in her hand, solely as a club. Susan let out one furious wail.

And Durham, moving more by instinct than by conscious thought, grabbed Wanbecq-ai's uplifted arm and pulled her over squalling onto his lap. Wanbecq started forward from the opposite seat.

"Don't," said Durham. He had Wanbecq-ai's wrist in one hand and her neck in the other, and he was not being gentle. Wanbecq-ai covered him, and the two of them together covered Susan. Wanbecq stood with his knees bent for a spring, his gun flicking back and forth uncertainly. Wanbecq-ai had stopped squalling. Her face was turning dark. Susan huddled where she is, half stunned. Durham shifted his grip on Wanbecq-ai's arm and got the gun into his own hand.

"Now," he said to Wanbecq. "Drop it."

Wanbecq dropped it. Durham scrabbled it in with his heel until it was between his own feet. Then he heaved Wanbecq-ai forcibly at her husband. It was like heaving a rag doll, and while Wanbecq was dealing with her Durham managed to pick up the other gun.

Susan lifted her head. She looked around with glassy eyes and then, with single-minded persistence, she got up. Durham said sharply, "Sit down!"

Susan reached up for the emergency. Durham smacked her across the stomach with the back of his left hand, not daring to take his eyes off the Wanbecqs. She doubled over it and sat down again. Durham said, "All right now, damn it, all of you sit still!"

*

The taxi sped on it humming rail, farther and farther into the reaches of the spaceport. Below there were the wide clear spaces of the landing aprons, and great ships standing in them, their tails down and their noses high in the air, high above the monorail, towering over the freight belts and the multitude of machines that served them.

Ahead there was the racing edge of twilight, and beyond it, coming swiftly, was the lunar night.

Durham said to Wanbecq, "What's this all about?"

Wanbecq sneered.

"You know," said Durham, "there's a law against changing the color of your skin for the purpose of committing criminal acts. That's so the wrong people won't get blamed. There's a law against carrying lethal weapons. There is even, humorously enough, a law against espionage on The Hub. You know I'm going to turn you over to the authorities?"

Again, Wanbecq sneered. He was a hateful little man, but he looked so young and so proudly martyred that Durham almost felt sorry for him. Almost. Not quite.

"On second thought," he said, "I guess I'll save you both for Jubb."

That was a random shot, prompted by the memory of how their faces looked when the shadow-thing had squealed that word at them. It hit. Wanbecq's face became distorted with a fanatic hatred, and Wanbecq-ai, rubbing her throat, croaked, "Then you are in league with The Beast." She pronounced that name with unmistakable capitals.

"Who said I was?" asked Durham. "The darkbird came to help you. It told us Jubb had claimed you."

"It did," said Durham softly, "did it?" The dark birds will soon fly. The dark birds merely refer to a couple of ships engaged in poaching. That's what you say, Mr. Hawtree.

"What is a dark bird? You mean that shadow thing

36

"They are the servants, the familiars of The Beast," said Wanbecq. "The instruments by which he hopes to enslave all humanity. Do not pretend, Mr. Durham."

"I'm not. This Jubb, what is he beside The Beast?"

Wanbecq stared at and Durham made a menacing gesture. "Come on, I want to know."

"Jubb is the ruler of Senya Dik."

"And Senya Dik?"

"Our sister planet. A dark and evil sister, plotting our destruction. A demon sister, Mr. Durham. Have you ever heard of the Bitter Star?"

"I never heard of any of it but I find it interesting. Go on."

"Whoever controls the darkbirds controls the Star, and whoever controls the Star can do anything he wishes. This is Jubb." Wanbecq thrust out his hands. "You're human, Mr. Durham. If you have sold your soul, take it back again. Fight with us, not against us."

"I assume," said Durham, "that Jubb is not human."

Wanbecq-ai made an abrupt sound of disgust. "This is silly, Mr. Durham. If you know so little, why are you going to Nanta Dik at all?"

Durham did not answer. He did not have any answer to that one. Wondered if ever he would have it.

"If you are so ignorant," continued Wanbecq-ai viciously, "of course you don't know that the Terran consul Karlovic is over his head in intrigue, conniving with Jubb in order to make this treaty of Federation." Durham sat up straight. "A treaty of what?"

"The sector," said Wanbecq slowly, "will belong either to the human race or to the beast, but it cannot belong to both."

"Federation," said Durham, answering his own question. And suddenly many formless things began to fit together into a shape that was still cloudy but had a sinister solidity. In order for a solar system to become a member of the Federation its member planets were required to have achieved unity among the common citizenship, a common council, common laws. And in order for a sub-sector to become federated, all its systems must have reached a like accord.

In this case, since the system of the two Diks was the only inhabited one in the sub-sector, the two things were the same.

The fate of 9G rested solely on the behavior of two planets.

If 9G remained unfederated, the company or companies engaged in mining or other business under local license could continue to operate in almost any way they chose as long as they kept the local officials happy. They could strip the whole area of its mineral resources, pile up incredible fortunes, and leave the native worlds with nothing. But if 9G became a member of the Federation, Federation law would immediately step in, and Federation enforcement of same, and if there were any abuses of native rights, the people responsible would suffer for it.

Postulate a company. Postulate a connection between it and Hawtree. Postulate and postulate.

At around three hundred miles an hour the taxi plunged into the twilight zone. Light sprang on automatically. Outside it became dark very swiftly, and the darkness roared, and glittered with a million lamps.

"Who," asked Durham, "is principally against your two worlds uniting so that the treaty can go through?"

"All of us," said Wanbecq fiercely. "Shall we give up our rights, our independence, our human institutions, everything our race has stood for."

Wanbecq-ai cried out, "We will never unite, never! No one can force us to betray our species!"

38

LEIGH BRACKETT

Susan began to cry.

"Please," said Durham. "Baby? You're all right."

"You hit me."

"I had to. I'll apologize later. Be quiet now, Susan, please." He turned back to the Wanbecqs. "Everybody on Nanta Dik feels that way?"

"There are traitors everywhere," said Wanbecq darkly. "Some of them, unfortunately, are in positions of power."

"They won't be for long," said Wanbecq-ai. "Look here, Mr. Durham, you're going to Nanta Dik with a message. We aren't the only ones who want to know what it is. Jubb has sent a darkbird for you. Take my advice. Tell us your message and back to The Hub."

Susan said in a nasty muffled voice, "You're insane. Nobody would trust him with a message to the milkman. He lost his job because he couldn't be trusted."

Without rancor, Durham said, "You're absolutely right, darling. And wouldn't it be strangely fitting if that's why I got my job back again?" He said to the Wanbecqs, "Somebody tipped you off about me. Who?"

"We know him only as a friend of humanity."

"Somebody must have sent you here from Nanta Dik."

"On our world there are many friends of humanity. Think of them, Mr. Durham, when you kiss the Bitter Star."

*

The taxi slowed, strongly, smoothly. The blurred panorama of lights and ships became separable into individual shapes. Durham stared out ahead. There was the form of a freighter, ugly and immensely powerful, on a landing apron only partially lighted. The Margaretta K.

Durham asked. "Who owns her?"

LAST CALL FROM SECTOR 9G

"Universal Minerals."

"And who owns Universal Minerals?"

"Several people, I think, all Earthmen."

"Who speaks for Universal Minerals on Nanta Dik?"

A little reluctantly, Wanbecq said "There is a man named Morrison."

The name rang no bell in Durham's mind. It brought no visible reaction to Susan's face either, though he was watching it closely.

"And how," he asked, "does Morrison feel about humanity?"

"Ask the Bitter Star," said Wanbecq, and the taxi slid to a halt beside the platform on which Durham now saw that several men were standing. Wanbecq and Wanbecq-ai hunched forward expectantly.

"No," said Durham. "I'm getting out, but you're not." He nudged Susan. "Get ready."

The doors slid open automatically. Susan scrambled out. Durham went right behind her, twisted like a cat in the opening, and splashed a brief warning blast off the floor at the feet of the Wanbecqs, who had raised a frantic cry and were trying to follow.

Susan aid breathlessly, "Oh!"

The men who had been standing on the platform were now rushing forward. Three were lean and butter-colored. One was a burly Earthman, who said in a tone of amazement, "What the hell!"

"Hold it!" Durham shouted. He swept Susan behind him and tried to cover all fronts at once, not knowing whether the men were there to capture him or were only there by chance and responding to the Wanbecqs' cry for help. "These people attacked us. I have passage on your ship!"

From out of the night there came a shrill, flat, hooting cry of "Jubb! Jubb! Jubb!"

The butter-colored men yelled. They scattered away and out, their feet scrabbling on the platform. The Earthman was slower and more belligerent. He turned around and the spiky little blob of darkness came leaping at him. He put up his hands and struck at it, and the darkbird hooted as the fists passed through it, crackling. The Earthman opened his mouth in a round shocked O and went rigid, rising up on the tips of his toes. The darkbird seemed to merge with his skull for the fraction of a second, and he crumpled down with his mouth still open and his chest rising and falling heavily. The darkbird swooped toward Durham.

Durham fired at it.

It soaked up part of the beam and left the rest, like a well-fed cat rejecting an overplus of milk. It darted past Durham and into the taxi, where it bounced agilely, once and twice. Wanbecq and Wanbecq-ai fell down on the floor. The doors closed softly, and the taxi mechanism whirred, and the rail hummed as it took off, heading back to the main terminal. The darkbird returned to Durham.

Susan said in a strange voice, "What is that?"

"Never mind now. Come on."

He started to drag her toward the ramp that led down from the platform. She fought him. She was getting hysterical, and he didn't blame her. The darkbird followed along behind. When they reached the level, Susan planted her feet mulishly and refused to go any farther.

"I don't dare leave you alone out here," he said desperately. "Come along to the ship and the captain will see that you get back safely."

The darkbird circled and dived at Susan. She bolted. It dived at Durham. He bolted too, off to the right, to the edge of the apron, where he caught up with Susan again. They ran between the storage sheds, onto a spur of the freight-belt system. It was still now, not carrying any freight. They tried to run across it to the other side, but the darkbird drove them back. It was immediately apparent, of course, that the thing was herding them. He shouted at it to let Susan alone, but it did not listen to him. And he thought, it wants us to go somewhere, so it won't knock us out. Maybe? It's worth a try.

He took Susan and jumped off the belt and ran.

The darkbird touched him, ever so gently. He tried to yell, gave up, and tottered back where it wanted him to go, with every nerve in him pulled taut and twangling in a horrible half-pleasurable fashion that made his legs and arms move unnaturally, as though he were dancing. The darkbird followed, once again placid and unconcerned.

They went along the belt for some distance. It was limber, sagging a bit between the giant rollers, and it boomed under their feet with a sharp slapping sound. Susan stumbled so often he picked her up and carried her. There was nobody to call to, nobody to ask for help. The towering ships were far away.

The darkbird nudged him again at last, out across a landing apron where a very strange looking ship stood in the solitary of majesty of impending take-off. The flood lights were blinking at twenty-second intervals, visual warning to stand clear, and Durham ran staggering through a stroboscopic nightmare, with the white-faced girl in his arms.

Dark, light. Black, bright. A haze of exhaustion swam before his eyes. Things moved in it, jerky shapes in an old film, in in antique penny peep show. Day, night. Dark, bright. The things moved closer, unhuman things clad in fantastic pressure suits. Durham screamed.

He tried to run again, and the darkbird touched him. Once more there was the unbearable twitching of the nerves and he danced in the black, bright, day, night. He danced into a large box that was waiting for him, and he kept going until he struck the end wall of hard metal. He turned then and saw the very thick door go sighing shut and the dogs go slipping into place snick-snick or the other, and it was too late even to try to get out again.

He set Susan down as gently as he could and sank down beside her. The floor moved up under him sharply. There was a clanging and clattering of tackle overhead, and then a sickening sidewise lurch. The on-off pattern of the light changed outside the two round windows that were in the box. It became a steady green, in which his hands showed like two sickly-white butterflies on his knees. There were more noises, hollow and far away, and then a second lurch, a lift, a drop, and after that a larger motion encompassing the box and the entire locus in which it stood.

Durham put his face in his hands and gave up.

CHAPTER V.

SUSAN was screaming. Let me out. She was pounding on something. Durham started up. He must have slept or passed out. The box was perfectly still now. There was no sense of motion. But he could tell by the change in gravity that the ship was in space.

Susan was by one of the windows. She was pounding on it with her favorite implement, the heel of her shoe. Durl went to her and glanced out. Cold sweat broke out on him, and he grabbed her hand.

"Stop it! Are you crazy?" He wrenched the shoe from her and threw it across the small space of the box. Then he felt of the glass, peering at it, frantic lest she should have cracked it.

"I'm going to get," said Susan grimly, and groped around for something heavier.

"Look." He shook her and turned her face to the window. "Do you see that air out there?"

The box now stood in a large empty hold. He could see the curve of the ship's hull, ribbed with tremendous struts of steel, and a deck of metal plates, glistening in the green light. Green light? Earth should have a yellow-white type light, the kind that the sun gives off. Well yes, but suppose that the sun was green?

Nanta Dik circles a green star.

So does Senya Dik. Those creatures outside the ship were anything but humanoid. Jubb's darkbird herded us in here. Easy. Now we know.

"What about the air?" asked Susan. "Let go of me."

"It's poisonous. Can't you tell by looking at it?" It rolled and roiled and sluggishly shifted in vapors of thick chartreuse and vivid green. "And don't you remember, they were wearing pressure suits? They couldn't live in our atmosphere. We surely couldn't live in theirs."

There was no answer.

45

"Susan. Susan?"

"I want to go home," she said, and began to cry.

"There now, Susie. Take it."

"Don't call me Susie!"

"All right, but take it easy. I'll find out what the situation is and then I'll..."

"You'll what? You'll make a mess of things just like you always have. You'll get me into more trouble, just like you got me into this. You're no good, Lloyd, and I wish I'd never seen you. I wish I'd never come to say good-bye!" She rushed to the window and began to pound on it again, this time with her fists.

Durham hauled her away and shook her until her jaw rattled together. "I'm sorry you came too," he said savagely. "You're the last person in the galaxy I'd pick to be in trouble with. A damned spoiled female with no honesty, no courage, no nothing but your father's position to trade on." He wrapped his arms tight around her. "Hell, this is no time to be quarrelling. Let's both keep our mouths shut. Come on, honey, we're not dead yet."

She choked a little and stood trembling against him. Then she said, "I think I fell over a chair a while ago. Maybe there's a lamp. Let's look."

The green light was dim, but their eyes were used to it. They found a lamp and turned it on. The box was flooded with a clear white glare, very grateful to Earthly senses. Durham looked around and said slowly, "I'll be damned."

The box was about the size of a small room. It had in it an armchair, a bunk, compact cupboards and lockers, a sink and hotplate, and a curtained-off corner with a sanitary device. Durham turned on one of the sink taps. Water came out. He turned it off and went and sat down in the armchair.

"I'm damned," he said again. "Freezer," said Susan, looking into things. "Food concentrates. Pots and pans. Blanket. Change of clothes, all men's. Booze, two bottles of it. Rack of micro-books. Somebody went to a lot of trouble."

"Yes."

"Pretty comfortable. Everything you need, all self-contained."

"Uh."

"But Lloyd, it's only for one." He said dismally, "We'll take turns on the bunk." But it wasn't the bunk that worried him. He went and looked out of the other window. By craning his head, he could see an assembly of storage tanks, pressure tanks, pumps, purifiers, blower units, all tightly sealed against any admixture of Senyan air. That, too, was only for one. A most ghastly claustrophobia came over Durham, and for a moment he saw Susan, not as a spoiled and pretty girl, but as his rival for the oxygen that was life.

Susan said, "Lloyd. Something is coming in."

For an instant he thought she meant into the box, and then he realized that the reverberating clang he heard must be the hatch door of the hold. He joined her at the opposite window.

There were two, no three dark shapes coming toward the box, moving swiftly through the green and chartreuse vapors. They undulated on two pairs of stubby legs set fore and aft under a flexible lower body. Their upper bodies, carried erect, were rather bulbous and tall, with well-defined heads and two sets of specialized arms, the lower ones thick and powerful for heavy work, the upper ones as delicate as an engraver's fine tools. Their skin was a glossy black, almost like patent leather. They wore neat harnesses of what looked like metal webbing in the way of dress, and on the breast strap each one carried an insigne.

"Ship's officers," Durham guessed. "Probably one of them is the captain."

"They're horrible," said Susan. She backed away from window until the end of the bunk caught her behind the knees and she sat down.

Durham laughed. "Fine pair of cosmopolites we are. We're used to the idea of non-humanoids. There are a lot of them on The Hub, but they're mostly segregated by necessity, so we practically never really see any. But now we're the ones who have to be segregated. And the reality is quite another thing from the idea, isn't it?"

*

He backed away himself, two, until shame made him stop. The three non-humanoids came and looked with large iridescent eyes, through the window. Their oddly shaped mouths moved rapidly, so he knew that they were talking, and their slender upper arms were as mobile and expressive as the hands of so many girls at a sorority tea. Then one of them turned and did something to the wall of the box, and suddenly Durham could hear them clearly. There was a speaker device beside the window. Durham sprang at it.

"Can you hear me? Can you hear me out there? Listen, you have no right to do this, you've got to take us back! Miss Hawtree is the daughter of..."

"Mr. Durham." The voice was unhuman but strong, and the Esperanto it spoke was perfectly understandable. "Please calm yourself and listen to what I have to say. I appreciate your feelings—"

"Hah!"

"But there is nothing I can do about it. I have my orders, and I can assure you—"

"From Jubb?"

"You'll be fully informed when you reach Senya Dik. Meanwhile, I can assure you that no harm will come to you, now or later. So please put your fears at rest. A little patience..."

Susan had leaped up. Now she flung herself upon the speaker mike. "What about me?"

"Your presence was unexpected, and I fear it's going to be rather difficult for you both. But you must make the best of it. In regard to air and water, I must caution you that the supply will hardly be adequate for you both unless you are extremely careful."

This had not occurred to Susan before.

"You mean?"

"I mean that you must use no more water than is absolutely necessary for drinking and preparing your food. The food you share between you, on half ration. As for the air..."

"Yes," said Durham. "What about the air."

"I believe that activity has the effect of increasing your metabolism, thereby consuming more oxygen. So, I would advise you both to move and speak as little as possible. Remain calm. Remain quiet. In that way you should be able to survive. It is not that we are grudging. It is simply that we cannot share any of our supplies with you, because you are alien life forms and totally incompatible. If we had known there would be two, we would have prepared. As it is, you must work together to conserve."

"But," said Susan, "but this isn't fair, it isn't right! You'll take me back or my father will see to it."

"Keep this speaker open," said the Senyan, "so that you will be sure to hear the audio signal, a sustained note repeated at intervals of forty seconds. Prepare to enter overdrive."

He did not say good-bye. He merely went away with his two officers. Susan screamed after them. Durham clapped his hand over her mouth and took her forcibly and put her on the bunk.

"Lie there," he said. "Quiet. Didn't you hear him? Don't move, don't talk."

He sat down in the chair, consciously trying not to breathe deeply.

"But..."

"Don't you say shut up to me, Lloyd-This is all your fault."

"My fault? Mine? Because you had to shove yourself in..."

"Shove myself? Father was right about you. And it is your fault. If you hadn't asked me to ride down with you..."

"Oh, shut up, damn it, that's just like a woman! If you knew your next breath was your last one, you'd still have to use it for talk. You want to asphyxiate us both with your gabbling?"

She was quiet for a long while. Then he realized that she was crying.

"Lloyd, I'm scared."

"So am I." He began to laugh. "When I come to think of it, it was your father that got us both into this. I hope he sweats blood in great gory streams."

"You're a drunken ungrateful swine! If dad really did give you another chance..."

"Ah, ah! Remember the oxygen! He did. And I was such a fatheaded idiot I thought it was on the level. I even reformed." He laughed again, briefly. "Overcome with gratitude, I did exactly what I was supposed not to do. I sobered up and held my tongue."

"I don't understand at all."

"I was supposed to talk, Susan. I was given a message, and I was supposed to babble it all over The Hub. I don't know exactly what that message was intended to trigger off when it got into circulation.

50

Probably a war. But I'll bet I know what I triggered off by not talking. Trouble for your old man."

"I don't believe a word of it."

Durham shrugged. It was very little effort to reach out and lift a bottle from a nearby cupboard. He opened it and took a long pull. Then he looked at the bottle, shook his head, and passed it to Susan.

She made a derisive noise, and he shrugged again.

"That's right. Funny thing. First, I was stricken with remorse and determined to be worthy. Now I'm just mad. Before I get through, I'm going to hang your father higher than Haman."

The audio signal, shrill and insistent and sounding somehow as unhuman as the voices of the Senyans, came piercingly through the speaker.

Susan gasped. "Wherever they're taking us, they're not going to kill us, are they?"

"I think they want to question us. I think some dirty work is going on, one of those million-credit-swindle things you hear about once in a while, and I think your father is right up to his neck in it. If I'm right, that's the chief reason you were brought along."

"I think you're a dirty low-down liar," she said, in a voice he could hardly hear.

The signal continued to squeal. Durham moved to the bunk. "Slide over."

"No."

But she did not fight him when he pushed himself in beside her and took her in his arms.

"The haughty Miss Hawtree," he said, and smiled. "You're a mess. Hair in your eyes. Make-up all smeared. Tears dripping off the end of your nose."

The light dimmed, became strange and eerie.

51

LAST CALL FROM SECTOR 9G

"They could have made this damned bunk a little wider."

"It doesn't matter. After a trip like this, I won't have any reputation left, anyway. Nobody would believe me on oath."

The fabric of the ship shifted, strained, slipped, moved. The fabric of Durham's body did likewise. He set his teeth and said, "Don't worry, dear. I can always ask the captain to marry us."

By the time the audio-signal shrilled again, heralding a return to solar system speeds and space, it seemed that ages had passed.

*

They did not talk about marriage now, even in jest. They hated each other! "Cabin fever," they had said politely for a while, making excuses. But they did not bother with excuses any more. They just had simply and quietly loathed each other, as the long, timeless time went by.

Pity, too, thought Durham, looking at Susan where she lay in the bunk. She's really a handsome wench, even without all the makeup and the hairdo and those incredible undergarments that women use, as though they were semi-liquescent. Just lying there in her slip now, she looks younger, gentler, nice and soft, as though she'd be pleasant to hold in your arms again if you had the strength and the oxygen and if you didn't hate her so.

"Lloyd?"

"Huh?"

"How long before we land?"

"How should I know?"

"Well, you could find out."

"You find out. You can yell as loud as I can. Louder."

"I'll yell," said Susan ominously. "The second I get out of here; I'll yell so loud the whole galaxy will hear me."

"I should think they've already heard you clear out to Andromeda."

52

The lights dimmed. The peculiar noises and wrenching's that went with coming out of overdrive began. Durham braced himself.

"It's too bad you reformed," said Susan. "You used to be amusing company, at least. Now you're sour and bad tempered. You're also..."

What he was also Durham never heard. There was a crashing, roaring, rending impact. The chair went out from under him so that he fell face up into the ceiling. The lights went out entirely. He heard a thin faint sound that might have been Susan screaming. Then the ceiling slid away from him and spilled him down a wall. As he went scrabbling past the window he looked out and saw that there were now long vertical rents in the outer hull through which the stars were shining. The pumps had stopped.

A long settling groan and then silence. The antigrav field was dead. Durham floated, along with everything else that was not bolted down.

"Susan," he said. "Susan?"

"Here."

They met and clung together in mid-air while the hull began a slow axial rotation around them.

"What happened?"

"We hit something."

"The Senyans?"

They must all be done for. The hull is split open. Head-on ram, I think, just as we came out of overdrive. They wouldn't have had time to get space armor."

"Then are we?"

"Hush. Don't talk. Just wait and see."

They clung together, silent. The hull turned without sound, and the stars shone in through the long slits, into the empty vacuum of the hold.

"Lloyd, I can't breathe."

"Yes, you can. We still have as much air as ever. It just isn't circulating now."

"I don't know if I can stand this, Lloyd. It's such an awful way."

"There isn't any way that's good. It won't be so bad, really. You'll just go off to sleep."

"Hold onto me?"

"Sure."

"Lloyd."

"What?"

"I'm sorry."

"So am I."

The hull turned and the stars glittered.

The vitiated air grew foul, grew thick and leaden. The man and woman floated in the closed space, their arms tight around each other, their faces close together.

Something jarred against the hull.

"Lloyd! I see a light!"

"It's only a star."

"No. Look through the window. Moving!"

Men, humans, wearing pressure suits, had come into the hull. Two of them were dragging oxygen bottles. They came up to the box and flashed their lights in through the windows. They knocked and made reassuring signs. After a minute or two fresh oxygen hissed in under pressure through the air duct. Susan laughed a little and then fainted. Durham still held her in his arms. Everything got pleasantly dark and far away, lost in the single simple joy of breathing.

There were sounds and motions, but he did not pay much attention to them, and he was mildly surprised when he happened to float past a window and noticed that now there was only space outside, very large and full of hot and splendid lights. When he passed the other window, he saw part of a ship, and he understood that the box was being hoisted across the interval between it and the wreck. It seemed a remarkably kind dispensation of fortune to have provided a ship at exactly the right time and place, and not just any ship but one equipped with the specialized tackle required for moving heavy loads in space.

A mighty cargo hatch swallowed the box. Susan came to, and they waited, weakly hysterical, Durham not even noticing that a spiky shadow had slipped in with the box. Suddenly again there was man-made light, and then the sound of heavy air pumps reached them. The pumps stopped, and, quite simply, men came in and opened the door of the box.

There was a considerable noise and confusion, everybody talking at once. Durham lost track of Susan. He was only partly conscious of what he was doing, but he felt that everybody was in a hurry to get something done. Then there was a cabin with a port in it, and beyond the port there was space, and in that space a great light flared blindingly and was gone

CHAPTER VI.

Morrison said, "Murder is a harsh word, Durham. After all, they weren't human."

"There's no such difference under Federation law"

"We're not under Federation law here."

"No. And you're engaged in a life-or-death struggle to make sure you don't come under it. This happened to be one of the death parts."

Morrison looked at him in mild surprise. "You figured that out, Durham?" He was a lean gray, kindly looking man, the conventional father type. Susan was staring at him in blank horror, as though she could not believe what she was hearing. "I wasn't told you were that bright. Well, you're right. Universal Minerals and its various dummy corporations in this sub-sector are making such profits as you wouldn't believe if I told you, and we have no intention of giving it up."

"Even if you have to slaughter a whole ship's crew. What did you do, tow an asteroid into position?"

Morrison shrugged. "Special debris is not uncommon."

"You could have killed us, too, you know," Durham said angrily. "You could have killed her. Hawtree wouldn't have liked that."

"It a risk we had to take. It was a small one." He looked Durham up and down. "You made us one whale of a mess of trouble. If my yacht wasn't a good bit faster than Jubb's ship, we'd have been whipped. What happened to you? Why didn't you talk like you were supposed to?"

"You'd die laughing."

"I can control my emotions. Go ahead." Durham told him. "Virtue," he finished sourly, "is sure enough its own reward. I should have stayed drunk. I was happier that way. What happened to the Wanbecqs?"

Morrison was still laughing. "They had not come to when their taxi reached the terminus. The port police picked them up." He took a bottle out of a locker and pushed it and a glass across the cabin table to Durham. "Here. You've earned it. Wait till I tell Hawtree. And he was so sure of you. Just goes to show you can't trust anybody."

Susan said, "But why?" Shock was making her mind move slowly. It was a minute before they realized she was referring to the Senyan ship.

She added, very slowly, "It's true about my father?"

"I'm afraid it is," said Morrison. "But I wouldn't worry about it too much. He's a very rich man. He's also a shrewd one, and it looks now as though he's going to be all right. Give her a drink, Durham, she needs it. Would you like to lie down, Miss Hawtree? All right, then, I'll tell you why."

He leaned over her with no look of kindness at all. "Get this all clearly in mind, Miss Hawtree, so you'll understand that if at any time you try to hang me, you'll hang your father too. We're partners, equally guilty. You understand that."

"Yes." She looked so white that Durham was frightened. But she sat quietly and listened.

"For years now," Morrison said, "I have managed the company here, and Hawtree has used his position with the Embassy to see that I have a free hand. He sees that no complaints get to ears higher up. He sees that any annoying red tape is taken care of. Most important of all, he sees that any official communication from either of the Diks that might be unfavorable to us is permanently lost in the files, including all requests for aid in achieving Federation status. Our connection, naturally, is one of the best kept secrets in the galaxy.

"We had very easy sailing until Jubb rose to power on Senya Dik. Jubb is an able leader. He knows what's happening to the resources of the sector, and he knows the only way to put a stop to it. Unfortunately for us, all the leaders on Nanta Dik aren't fools either, and there is a growing movement toward unification. Jubb has pushed it and pushed it, so that we've been forced to take more and more vigorous steps. The human supremacy groups, made up of such people as the Wanbecqs, have been very useful. And of course, Senya Dik has its lunatic fringe too, in reverse but equally useful. But Jubb started a campaign of petitioning the Embassy. He poured it on so hard that Hawtree knew he wasn't going to be able to pigeonhole all the petitions forever. Furthermore, it was obvious that Jubb knew there must be collusion somewhere and was hammering away to find it. So Hawtree sent for me."

"And," said Durham, "you said, 'Let's start a war between the two planets. Then unification can't possibly take place, and Jubb will have too much on his hands to bother us.' Maybe he'll even be eliminated. And you went looking for a goat."

"Exactly. You were given a message about dark birds that would have significance only to a Nantan. The Wanbecqs were put on your trail. All you had to do was talk."

"What if I had talked too much?"

"How could you? You didn't know anything. And Hawtree's story would be that he had simply given you passage home, which you had bought."

"And anyway," said Durham thoughtfully, "I would have been either dead in an alley somewhere, or aboard a ship going to Nanta Dik, which I would not have reached."

"It was a flexible situation."

Susan said, "Then you admit that you..." She could not finish.

LAST CALL FROM SECTOR 9G

Morrison turned on her irritably. "You very nearly wrecked us, Miss Hawtree. Durham's disappearance wouldn't have raised a ripple, but the daughter of a highly placed diplomat vanishing was quite another thing. Your father had to think fast and talk faster, or public curiosity would have forced an investigation right then. Fortunately, the Wanbecqs helped. They painted a pretty dark picture of Jubb, and Hawtree was able to smooth things over since everybody knew you'd been sweet on Durham and had obviously gone to say good-bye. Hawtree did such a good job, in fact, that he had the whole Hub seething with indignation against Jubb even before I left. So, it turned out well, in spite of you."

"But why did you have to wreck the ship?"

"Well, we had to get you back. We couldn't let Jubb have Mr. Durham to use as a witness against us, and we certainly couldn't let him have Hawtree's daughter to use as a club over Hawtree. Now, you see, the situation is this."

He nodded to the cabin port beyond which the bright flare had come and gone, leaving nothing but emptiness.

"There's nothing left of the ship but atoms, and no one can say what happened to it. Jubb does not have you two, but he can't prove it as long as you're kept out of sight. So, we keep you out of sight, and at the same time press demands to Jubb for your return. It looks as though he's hiding you, or has killed you, in fear of the storm he has raised. The more he doesn't give you up the more human opinion turns against him, and the more his own people figure he's made them nothing but trouble. Meanwhile, the Wanbecqs are on their way home with a big story. We can still have our war if we want it. And Jubb's days are numbered."

Durham said slowly, "What if he decides to use the Bitter Star?"

Morrison stared at him, and then laughed. "Don't try to frighten me with my own bogeyman. I took a story a thousand years old and resurrected it and talked it up until it caught. But that's all it is, a story."

"Are you sure? And what about the dark-birds? They seem to get around. Won't they tell Jubb where we are?"

"He'd have a hard time proving it on the word of a shadow. Besides, there are defenses against them. They won't interfere."

"I suppose," said Durham, taking the bottle into his hand as though to pour again, "that it wouldn't bother you to know that one of them is in here now."

Morrison did not take his eyes from Durham's face. "Hawtree made a stinking choice in you. Put down that bottle."

Durham grinned. He raised the bottle higher and chanted, "Jubb, Jubb, Jubb!"

Morrison said between his teeth, "This would have had to be done anyway." Still watching Durham, he reached one swift hand into the belt of his tunic. Susan made a muffled cry and started to get up. None of the motions were finished. A shadow came out from the darkness of a corner behind Morrison's chair. It flicked against him and he fell across the table, quite still. The darkbird came and hung in the air in front of Durham.

"Jubb," it said.

Durham put down the bottle and wiped the sweat off his forehead. He looked at the dark bird, feeling cold and hollow. "I want to go to him. You understand? To Jubb."

Up and down it bounced, like the nodding of a head.

Susan said, "What are you going to do?"

"Try and steal a lifeboat."

"I'm going with you."

"No. Morrison doesn't want to kill you, but don't push him too far. You stay. Then if I don't make it you'll still be ..."

He broke off. "That's taking a lot for granted, isn't it? After all, Hawtree is your father."

She whispered, "I don't care."

"It's the biggest decision you'll ever make. Don't make it too fast." He kissed her. "Besides, if you wait, you may not have to make it at all."

He took Morrison's gun and went out, and the darkbird went with him, bunched small and darting so swiftly that the two men it struck down never saw it. Durham turned aside into the communications room, and the darkbird saw to it that there was no alarm. He damaged radio and radar so that it would take some time to fix them. Then he went on down the corridor to the plainly marked hatch that led to Lifeboat No. 1. He got into it, with the dark bird. As soon as the boat hatch itself was shut, automatic relays blew him free of the pod on a blast of air.

"Jubb," said the dark bird. It touched him, and to his amazement there was no shock, only a chilly tingling that was not unpleasant. Then it simply oozed out through the solid hull, the way smoke oozes through a filter, and was gone.

Durham had no time for any more astonishments. The controls of the lifeboat were designedly very simple and plainly marked.

Durham got himself going and away from Morrison's ship as fast as he could. But be knew that it was not going to be anything like fast enough if the darkbird didn't hurry.

It hurried. And Durham was closer to Senya Dik than he realized. In less than three hours he was in touch with a planetary patrol ship, following it in toward the green blaze of KL421, and a dim cool planet that circled it, farther out than the orbit of Earth around Sol, but not quite so far as Mars.

CHAPTER VII.

THE spaceport was in a vast flat plain. Far across the plain Durham could see the dark outline of a city. He stood at the edge of the landing area, between two Senyan officers from the ship. He wore a pressure suit from the lifeboat's equipment, and the wind blew hard, beating and picking and pushing at the suit and the bubble helmet. It was difficult for Durham to stand up, but the Senyans, braced on their four sturdy legs, stood easily and swayed their upper bodies back and forth like trees.

They were big. He had not really understood how big they were until he stood beside them. He gathered that they were waiting for a ground conveyance, and he was not surprised. Light air cabs were hardly suited to their build.

He had talked briefly to Karlovic by radio, and he was impatient to get to the consulate where Karlovic was waiting for him. The minute or two in which they waited for the truck seemed interminable. But it came, a great powerful thing like a moving van, and one of the Senyans said,

"Permit me?"

With his two lower arms he lifted Durham onto the platform. The two Senyans spoke to the driver and then got on themselves. The truck took off, going very fast in spite of its size. The Senyans held Durham between them, because there was nothing for a human to hang to, and nowhere to sit down.

They left the spaceport. Huge storage buildings lined the road, and then smaller buildings, and then patches of open country, inexpressibly dreary to Durham's eyes. High overhead the sun burned green and small in a sky of cloudy vapor from which fell showers of glinting rain. Poison rain from a poison sky. Durham shivered, and

63

a deep depression settled on him. Nothing hopeful would be done in this place. Not by humans.

The truck roared on. Durham watched the city grow on the murky horizon, rising up into huge ugly towers and blocky structures like old prisons greatly magnified. It was a big city. It was a frightening city. He wished he had never seen it. He wished he was back in The Hub, standing on a high walk with the good hot sun pouring on him and no barriers between him and the good clean air. He wanted to weep with mingled weariness and claustrophobia. Then he noticed that little crowds had collected along the way into the city. They shouted at the truck going by, and waved their arms, and some of them threw stones that rattled off the sides.

"What's the matter?" Durham asked.

"They are members of the anti-human party. Prejudice cuts both ways, a thing our neighbors of Nanta Dik do not seem to understand. Human and non-human are intellectual concepts. On the emotional level it is simply us or not-us. You are not-us, and as such quite distasteful to some. What I do not understand is how they knew you were coming."

"Morrison must have got his radio working. He's been using the extremists here just like the ones on Nanta Dik, to make trouble."

"There are times ..." said the Senyan grimly. "But then I make myself remember that there are scoundrels among us, too."

The truck rumbled through the traffic of wide boulevards, between rows of massive buildings that had obviously never been designed with anything so small and frail as human beings in mind. There were Senyans on the streets, apparently going about whatever business they did, and Durham wondered what their home life was like, what games the children played, what they ate and how they thought, what things they worried about in the dark hours of the night. He felt absolutely alien. It was not a nice feeling.

Presently the truck turned into an open circle surrounded by mighty walls of stone.

In one place bright light shone cheerfully from the windows, and the Senyan said, "That is the consulate."

They set him off and showed him where the airlock was. Durham performed the ritual of the lock chamber, frantic to get out of the confining suit. When the inner door swung open, he began to tear at the helmet, and a man came in saying, "Let me help."

When Durham was free of the suit, the man looked at him with very tired, very angry eyes. "I'm Karlovic. Jubb's waiting. Come on."

He led Durham down an echoing corridor that dwarfed them by its size. The colors of the polished wood and stone were not keyed to the glaring yellow light, and the rooms that Durham could see into as he passed were not keyed to the small incongruous furnishings that had been forced upon them. Somewhere below there was a throbbing of pumps, and the air smelted of refresher chemicals.

Durham said, "You knew I was being brought here, didn't you?"

Karlovic nodded. "You, yes. The girl, no. She was an overzealous mistake on the part of the dark bird. Yes, I was in on it. I hoped that finally we could get proof, a witness against whoever in the Embassy was working with Morrison. Hawtree, is it? I'm glad to know his name."

He pushed open a door. The room beyond it was only half a room, cut in the middle by a partition of heavy glass. On the other side of the glass wall was the thick green native air, and three Senyars, one of whom came forward when Durham and Karlovic came in. A darkbird hovered close above him. He said to Durham, "I am Jubb"

There were communicator discs set in the glass. Jubb motioned Durham to a chair beside one. "First let me offer the apology that is due you. You were carrying a message which was not true, which would have made the people of Nanta Dik believe that we were about to come against them with the Bitter Star. The darkbirds warned me, and I felt that I had no choice. I could not let that message be delivered."

Durham said, "No one could blame you for that."

"You understand, I had another motive, too."

"Yes. I don't think you could be blamed for that, either."

*

Jubb looked at him with his large inscrutable eyes, totally alien, unmistakably intelligent. "I didn't know what you would be like, Mr. Durham, whether you would be in sympathy with your employers or not. Now of course it is evident that you can't be."

Durham said quietly, "I've been to a lot of trouble already to put a rope around their necks. I'm ready to go to a lot more. They've used me like ..." He could not think of the right word. Jubb nodded.

"Contempt is not an easy thing to take. I know. Then you will help?"

"In any way I can."

"I want you to go back with me to The Hub, Mr. Durham. Before, I was helpless without proof. Now, as head of a planetary government, I can insist on seeing the ranking Ambassador himself, and I can bypass Hawtree now that I know who he is. I want you to be my witness."

"Nothing," said Durham, "would please me more."

"Good," said Jubb. "Good. Karlovic, it looks as though the end of our long fight may be in sight at last. Take good care of Mr. Durham. He is more precious than gold.

"Meanwhile, Morrison had made us a problem on transportation. We provided that particular ship for the consul's comfort, when there was reason for him to travel in our territory, and we had planned to refit it so that it would accommodate two on the return journey. Now I must ask a ship from our friends on Nanta Dik, and that may take a little time. So, rest well, Mr. Durham."

He went out, and Karlovic led Durham back into the hall and from there into a tall gloomy chamber that had a shiny little kitchen lost in one corner of it. There was a table and chairs. Durham sat down and watched Karlovic busy himself with packages of food.

"You don't look very happy about all this," he said.

"I'm not unhappy. I'm worried."

"About what? Morrison can't do thing now."

"No? Listen, Mr. Durham, the emperors of Rome only ruled part of one little world, but they didn't give it up easily. Morrison won't, either. Remember, things are so bad for him now they can't possibly get any worse, only better."

Durham looked out the window. It was a double one, with a vacuum between the panes and protective mesh on the outside. The green air pressed thick against it. The sun had wheeled far over, and the shadows of the buildings were long and black.

"Do you stay here much?" he asked.

"I have lately," said Karlovic. "I had to. My life wasn't safe on Nanta Dik. You've no idea how high their feelings run there, thanks to Morrison." He began to set the table. Durham made no move to help. He was tired. He watched the shadows lengthen and fill the circle of lofty walls with their darkness.

"Couldn't the government there protect you?"

"Only part of the government wants to. And Morrison is working hard to frighten them with all this propaganda about the Bitter Star."

LAST CALL FROM SECTOR 9G

"Propaganda. That's what he said. Is it?"

"Absolutely - as far as the Senyans using it is concerned. But the thing itself is real. It's in the city here. I've seen it."

Karlovic put the heated containers on the table and sat down. He began methodically to eat.

"It's kind of a weird story. Probably it could only have happened on a world like this, with a totally non-human, bio-chemical set-up. Senyan science started early and advanced fast, a good deal faster than it did on Nanta Dik, for some reason. They did a lot of experimenting with solar energy and atomics and the forces that lie just on the borderline of life - or maybe intelligence would be a better word."

"Aren't the two more or less synonymous?"

"A hunk of platinum sponge or a mess of colloids can be intelligent, but never alive. The Star is. The darkbirds are. They're not matter, they're merely a nexus of interacting particles. But they live and think."

"What about the Star?"

"The scientists were trying for an energy matrix that would absorb solar power and store it like a battery. Something slipped, and the result was the Bitter Star. It absorbs solar power, all right, but in the form of heat, and it will take heat from anything. And it doesn't give it up. It merely absorbs more and more until every living thing near it is frozen and there's no more heat to be had. The Senyan scientists didn't know quite what to do with this thing they had created, but they didn't want to destroy it, either. It had too many angles they wanted to study. So they made the darkbirds, on the same pattern but without the heat-hunger, and with a readier intelligence, to be a bridge between themselves and the Star, to control it. They studied the thing until it proved too dangerous, and they prisoned it by

68

simply starving it at a temperature of absolute zero. So it has stayed ever since, but the darkbirds still guard it in case anything should happen to free it again. They almost seem to love it, in some odd un-fleshly way."

Durham frowned. "Then it could be used against Nanta Dik."

"Oh yes," said Karlovic somberly. "In fact, it was, once. The Star shone in their sky in midsummer and the crops blackened, the rivers froze, and men died where they stood in the fields. The Senyans won the war. That was a thousand years ago, but the Nantans never quite forgot it."

He got up and went morosely to the sink, carrying dishes. "I keep telling Jubb he ought to get rid of the thing. It's a sore point. But ..."

Somewhere below there was a very loud noise. The floor rose up and then settled again. Almost at once the air was full of dust, and an alarm bell began a strident ringing. Karlovic's mouth opened and closed twice, as though he was trying to say something. He let the dishes fall clattering around his feet, and then he ran with all his might out of the room and along the hall.

Durham followed him There was now no sound at all from below. The pumps had stopped.

Karlovic found his tongue. "Cover your face. Don't breathe."

*

Durham saw a thin lazy whorl of greenish mist moving into the hall. He pressed his handkerchief over his mouth and nose and made his legs go, hard and fast. He was right on top of Karlovic when they stumbled into the airlock. It was still clear.

They helped each other into their suits, panting in the stagnant air. Then, through the helmet audio, Durham could hear sounds from outside, muffled shouts and trampling. Karlovic went back into the consulate where the green mist was already clinging around his knees and looked out a window into the circle. Over his shoulder Durham could see Senyans milling around and he thought they were rioters, but Karlovic said, "It's all right, they're Jubb's guards."

They went back to the airlock, and from there into the open circle. Senyans escorted them hastily into the adjoining building, and Durham saw that guard posts were being set up. There was a gaping hole in the side of the consulate and the pavement was shattered, and there were pieces of machinery and stuff lying around. Durham figured rapidly in his head how much oxygen he had in his suit pack, and how long it would take to repair the consulate and get the air conditioning working again, and how long it would be before a ship could get here from Nanta Dik. He looked at Karlovic, whose face was white as chalk inside his helmet.

"The lifeboat," he said. Karlovic nodded. Some color came back into his face. "Yes, the lifeboat. We can live in it until the ship comes." He ran his tongue over his lips as though they were very dry. "Didn't I tell you Morrison wouldn't give up easy? Oh lord, the lifeboat!" He began to jabber urgently at the Senyans in their own tongue, and again his expression was agonized. Durham didn't need to be told what he was thinking. If anything happened to that lifeboat, they were two dead men on a world where humans had no biological right to be.

They were brought into a room where Jubb was busy with a bank of communicators and a batch of harried aides. The room was enormous, but it did not dwarf the Senyans, and the somber colors did not seem depressing in their own light. Jubb said, as they came in the door, "I've had a heavy guard set on your lifeboat. I don't think anyone can repeat that hit-and-run bombing ..." He cursed in a remarkably human fashion, naming Morrison and the Senyan fools who let themselves be used. "You are all right, Karlovic - Mr.

Durham? Quite safe? I've ordered a motor convoy. There are signs of unrest all over the city - apparently word has gone out that you, Durham, are carrying the unification agreement for my signature, and that the terms are a complete surrender on our part to human rule. Does it cheer you two to know that the human race is not alone in producing fools and madmen? Once on the spaceport you will be safe, my naval units will see to that, and my troops are already in the streets. They have orders to look out for you. Go with fortune."

They were taken out another way, where three heavy trucks and several smaller vehicles were drawn up. The Senyans in them wore a distinctive harness and were armed, and the vehicles all had armor plated bodies. Durham and Karlovic were lifted into one of the trucks, which was already filled with Senyan soldiers. The convoy moved off.

Durham braced himself in a corner and looked at Karlovic. "Happened fast, didn't it? Awfully fast."

"Violent things always do. You're not much used to violence, are you? Neither am I. Neither are most people. They get it shoved at them."

"I don't think we're through with it yet," said Durham.

Karlovic said, "I" told you."

For some time, there was only the rushing and jolting of the truck, the roar of motors and a kind of dim uneasy background of sound as though the whole city stirred and seethed. Durham was frightened. The food he had eaten had turned against him, he was stifling in his own sweat, and he thought of Morrison cruising comfortably somewhere out in space, smoking cigarettes and drinking good whiskey and sending down a message now and then, the way a man pokes with a stick at a brace of beetles, stirring them casually toward death.

LAST CALL FROM SECTOR 9G

He ground his jaws together in an agony of hate and fear, and the taste of them was sour in his mouth.

Somebody said to them, "We're on the spaceport highway now. It won't be long." A minute later somebody shouted and Karlovic caught the Senyan word and echoed it. "Barricade!" The truck rocked and whirled about and there were great crashes in the night that had fallen. Durham was thrown to his knees. The truck raced at full speed. There were sounds of fighting that now rose and now grew faint, and the truck lurched and swerved, and then there were more roars and crashes and it came violently to a halt. The Senyans began firing out of the loopholes in the armored sides. Some of them leaped out of the truck, beckoning Durham and Karlovic to come after them. A large force of rioters was attacking what remained of the convoy, which had been forced back into the city! Four of the Senyan soldiers ran with the two men into a side street, but a small body of rioters caught up with them. The soldiers turned to fight, and Karlovic said in a that was now curiously calm,

"If we're quick enough they may lose sight of us in the darkness."

He turned into an areaway between two buildings, and then into another, and Durham ran beside him through the cold green mist and the dim glow of lamps that glimmered on the alien walls. The sound of the fighting died away. They turned more corners, hunting always for the darkest shadows, hoping to meet a patrol. But the streets were deserted, and all the doors barred tight. Finally, Durham stopped. "How much oxygen you got left?" Karlovic peered at the illuminated indicator on the wrist of his suit. "Hour. Maybe less."

Both men were breathing hard, panting, burning up the precious stuff of life. Durham said, "I won't last that long. Listen, Karlovic. Where is the Bitter Star?"

Karlovic's face was a pale blur inside his helmet. "You crazy? You can't "

Durham put his two hands on the shoulders of Karlovic's suit and leaned his helmet close so that it clicked on Karlovic's.

"Maybe I'm crazy. In thirty, forty minutes I'll be dead, so what will it matter then? Listen, Karlovic, I want to live." He pointed back the way they had come. "You think we can walk through that to the spaceport in time?"

"No."

"We got anyplace else to go?"

"No."

"All right then. Let's give 'em hell."

"But they're not all our enemies. Jubb, my friends ..."

"Friend or enemy, they'll clear the way, we might just make it. Karlovic. You said the darkbirds control it, and you can talk to them." He shook Karlovic viciously. "Where is it? Don't you understand? If we use it we can hound Morrison out of space!"

Karlovic turned and began to walk fast, sobbing as he went. "The darkbirds will never let us. You don't know what you're doing."

"I know one thing. I'm sick of being pushed, pushed, pushed, into corners, into holes, where I can't breathe. I'm going to ..." He shut his teeth tight together and walked fast beside Karlovic, starting at every sound and shadow.

By twining alleys and streets where nothing moved for fear of the violence that was abroad that night, Karlovic led Durham to an open space like a park with vast locked gates that could keep a Senyan out but not a little agile human who could climb like a monkey with the fear of death upon him. Beyond the gates great wrinkled lichens as tall as trees grew in orderly rows, and a walk led inward. The lichens bent and rustled in the wind, and Durham's suit was wet with a poisonous dew.

The walk ended in a portico, and the portico was part of a building, round and squat as though a portion of its mass was underground. They passed through a narrow door into a place of utter silence, and a darkbird hung there, barring their way.

"Jubb," said Durham. "Tell it Jubb has sent us. Tell it the Bitter Star must be freed again to destroy Jubb's enemies."

Karlovic spoke to the shadow. Others came to join it. There was a flurry of ting and chittering, and then the one Karlovic had been speaking to disappeared in the uncanny fashion of its kind. The others stayed, a barrier between the two men and a ramp that led steeply down.

Karlovic sat down wearily on the chill stone. "It isn't any use," he said. "I knew it wouldn't be. The darkbird has gone to ask Jubb if what we say is true."

Durham sat down, too. He did not even bother to look at the indicator on his wrist. No use. The end. Finish. He shut his eyes.

There was a stir and a hooting in the air. Karlovic gasped. Then he began to shake Durham, laughing like a woman who has heard a risqué story.

"Didn't you hear? The bird came back, and Jubb said ... - Jubb said Morrison has been preaching the war of the Bitter Star, so let him have it."

He grasped Durham's suit by the shoulders and pulled him to his feet, and they ran with the cloud of shadows, down into the dimness below.

CHAPTER VIII.

There was a small sealed chamber with a thick window, and beyond it was a circular space, not too large, walled with triple walls of glass with a vacuum between. The air was full of darkbirds, moving without hindrance through the walls or hovering where they chose, above the thing that slept inside.

Durham blinked and turned his head away, and then looked back again. And Karlovic said softly, "Beautiful, isn't it? But sad, too, somehow, I don't know why."

Durham felt it, a subliminal feeling without any reason to it, like the sadness of a summer night or of birth and laughter or of gull's wings white and swift against the sky. The Star shone, palely, gently. He tried to see if it was round or any other shape, if it was solid or vaporous, but he could not see anything but that soft shining, like mist around a winter moon.

Durham shook himself and wondered why, when he was already so sure of death, he should be so afraid. "All right," he said. "How is it freed?"

"The darkbirds do that. Watch."

He spoke to them, one word, and in the glass-walled prison there was a stirring and a swirling of shadows around the soft shining of the Star. Durham saw a disc set in the metal overhead. One of the darkbirds touched it. There was an intense blue flare of light, and Durham felt the throbbing of hidden dynamos, a secret surge of power. The glass walls darkened and grew dim, the low roof turned and opened to the sky. And through the barrier window, Durham watched the waking of a star.

He saw the frosty shining brighten and spread out in slow unfurling veils. There was a moment when the whole building seemed filled with moon fire as cold as the breath of outer space and as beautiful as the face of a dream, and then it was gone, and the darkbirds were gone with it.

"Come on," said Karlovic, a harsh incongruous voice in the stunned darkness that was left behind, and Durham came, up the ramp and out into the parklike space beyond, and all the tall lichens were standing dead and sheathed in ice.

High above, burning cold over the city, a new star shone.

They followed it, through a silence as deep as the end of the world. Everything had taken cover at the rising of that star, and only the two men moved, the thermal units of their suits turned on high, through streets all glazed with ice and cluttered here and there with the wreckage and the dead of the rioting. The darkbirds were forcing the Star to stay high, but even so nothing could live long without protection in that sudden, terrible winter. The road to the port lay blank and bare. They found one of the smaller vehicles, its driver dead beside it. Karlovic got it going, moving the great levers with Durham's help. After that they rushed faster through the empty night. Durham shut his eyes, thinking.

He opened them, and the spaceport of Senya Dik lay black and deserted around him, and Karlovic was gasping to him for help. Together they pulled down the lever that stopped their conveyance. They scrambled down and ran out toward the small lifeboat, slipping and stumbling, dying inside their suits. They fell into the airlock, and Durham slammed the door and spun the wheel, waiting out the agonizing seconds while the tiny chamber cleared and then refilled, and they could tear off their helmets and breathe again. They looked at each other and la and hugged each other, laughed again and then went in to the cabin.

The communicator was flashing its light and burring stridently.

Durham switched it on. Jubb's face appeared in the tiny screen. "You are safe? Good, good. For a moment I thought ...! Listen. I have word from my patrol that Morrison has other ships with him now, spread out to catch you if by chance you get through. That is what decided me to use the Bitter Star. I am angry, Karlovic. I am tired of mockery and lies and secret violence. I am tired of peace which is only a cloak for another man's aggression."

A darkbird came into the cabin and hung over Durham's shoulder. "It will carry your messages," said Jubb. "I am leaving now for the port, and my own flagship. We go together. Good luck."

The screen went dead. Durham said, "Strap in, we're taking off."

* * *

The Star, with its herding pack of shadows, set a course that took them steeply up out of Senya Dik's shadow, into the full flood of the green sun's light. The dark-bird spoke by Durham's shoulder, and Karlovic said, "The Star must feed, or recharge itself, as you would say, with solar heat. Watch it, Durham. Watch it grow."

He watched. The Star spread out its misty substance, spreading it wide to the sun, and the soft shining of it brightened to an angry glare that grew and widened and became like a burning cloud, not green like the sunlight but white as pearl.

Far off to one side of it, Durham saw the glinting of a ship's hull. He pointed to it.

Karlovic worked with the communicator. In a minute the screen lit up, and Morrison's face was in it.

"Hello, Morrison," he said. "Hello, thief."

Morrison's face was as hard and white as something carved from bone.

"It wasn't just an old wives' tale, Morrison," he said. "It was true, and here it is. The Bitter Star, Morrison."

LAST CALL FROM SECTOR 9G

Karlovic reached over and shook him, pointing out the viewport. Coming swiftly in toward them was a small ship, curiously shaped before.

"Space-sweep," Karlovic said. "Those funny bulges are torpedo tubes, and the torpedoes carry heavy scatter charges to clear away debris so the ore ships can come in. "

Durham said to the image in the screen, "Call him off."

Morrison showed the edges of his teeth, and asked, "Why should I?"

Durham nodded to Karlovic, who spoke to the darkbird. It disappeared. Within a few seconds the Star had begun to move. It moved fast, the angry gleaming of its body making a streak like a white comet across the green-lit void. It wrapped itself around the space-sweep, and then it lifted, and the ship continued on its way unchanged. Morrison laughed.

The sweep rushed on toward the lifeboat. Its tubes were open, but nothing came out of them. Durham shifted course to clear it, and it blundered on by. In the screen, Morrison's image turned and spoke to someone, and the someone answered, "I can't, they just aren't there."

Morrison turned again to Durham, or rather to the image of him that was on his own screen. "I know what I'm supposed to say now, but I'm not going to say it. I I've got Miss Hawtree with me, had you forgotten that? I don't think you've suddenly acquired that kind of guts."

Durham shook his head. "I don t need them. I want you alive, Morrison. But I don't give a tinker's damn what happens to anybody else in this whole backside of nowhere you call 9G. Nobody and nothing. And I have the Bitter Star to back me up. I am wondering how many loyal employees of Universal Minerals, and how many stupid Wanbeqs are going to sacrifice their lives just to keep me from getting my hands on you. Call them up, Morrison, and count them out, and we'll send the Star to see them."

The Star glowed and glimmered and crew to a great shining, and a look of worry deepened on Karlovic's face. Morrison did not answer, and Durham could see the thoughts going around in his mind, the possibilities being weighed and evaluated. Then the someone who was behind Morrison and out of scanner range said in a queer flat voice,

"The tug Varmey calling in, sir. They boarded the sweep."

"Well?"

"All dead, sir. Frozen. Ever the air was frozen. They said to tell you they're going home."

"All right," said Morrison softly. "Durham, I'm going home too, to Nanta Dik. Let's see if you can follow me there."

He broke contact. In the distance Durham saw the bright speck that was Morrison's ship make a wheeling curve and speed away. Durham said grimly to Karlovic, "Tell the darkbirds to follow with the Star. And then get hold of somebody on Nanta Dik, somebody with authority. Tell them everything that's happened. Tell them Morrison is all we want. We'll see how close they let him get to home."

"I don't know," said Karlovic, busy with the communicator. Half an hour later he sighed and blanked the screen. "They're sending up a squadron to intercept Morrison. But they're scared. They're scared of the Star. I've promised them and nothing had better happen, Durhan."

Durham said. "We'd better send word to Jubb."

For what seemed an eternity they fled through the green blaze of the sun, after the ship Durham could no longer see. And ahead of the lifeboat, a light and a portent in the void, went the Bitter Star with its attendant shadows. And Durham, too, began to worry, he was not sure why. Jubb's flagship closed up to them, a vast dark whale beside a minnow. And after a while a tiny bright ball that was a planet came spinning toward them. Karlovic pointed.

Hung like a net across space, between them and the planet, was a series of glittering metallic flecks.

"The squadron."

The communicator buzzed. Karlovic snapped it on, and the face of a Nantan officer appeared on the screen.

"We have Morrison," he said. "Come no closer with the Star."

Karlovic spoke to the darkbird. Durham's hands, heavy with weariness, slowed the lifeboat until it hung almost motionless. Jubb's great dark cruiser slowed also. Above and between them burned the Bitter Star. It had ceased to move.

Durham said, "The Star will come no closer. "

"Mr. Karlovic," said the Nantan. "Bring your lifeboat in slowly, and alone."

The lifeboat came in among the ships or the squadron.

"Now," said the Nantan officer, "withdraw the Star."

Karlovic said, "Jubb will do so ..."

"No," said Durham suddenly, "Jubb will not. Look there!"

*

Shining with a furious light, the Star had torn itself away from the clustering shadows that hung around it.

Durham's heart congealed with a foretaste of icy death. The face of the Nantan officer paled, and Karlovic said in a voice that was not like his voice at all. "I must talk to Jubb."

He reached out to shift their single screen, and the Nantan officer said "Wait he is speaking on our alternate. I can adjust the scanner..."

The picture flopped, blurred, and cleared again, showing now in addition to the officer a part of the Nantan's alternate-channel screen. Jubb was speaking, and it seemed to Durham that the Senyan's strange face was clearly, humanly alarmed.

He said, "I cannot withdraw the Star. No, this is not a lie, a trick - hold your fire, you idiots! I'm the only hope you have now. The Star has profited by the lesson of its docility a thousand years ago, when it let itself be led back into captivity. Now it has grown too much. It cannot be brought back to any world."

Durham looked out at the beautiful deadly thing blazing so splendidly in the void. Can it be destroyed?"

"The darkbirds can destroy it," said Jubb. "If they will."

The Nantan officer, speaking from lips the color of ashes, said to the image of Jubb on the screen, "You have one minute to get it out of here before I fire "

Jubb turned his face away and spoke to something they could not see.

Durham turned to Karlovic. "He said, 'If they will' Does that mean—"

"I told you," said Karlovic, looking out the port, "that the darkbirds were created to guard the Star. And that, in a way they love it. Who can say how much?"

They watched.

Out in space the little cloud of darkbirds moved toward the Star. Then, hesitantly, they stopped.

"They won't," said Karlovic, in a whisper. Not even for Jubb."

Again, Jubb spoke to the unseen messenger, as quietly as though it was a casual order. And presently a troubled movement rippled the swirling darkbirds.

LAST CALL FROM SECTOR 9G

Suddenly they moved, again herding the Star Slowly at first, then more and more swiftly until it was only a streak of brilliant light, the darkbirds drove the Star straight toward the sun. And it was less a driving than an urging, a tempting, a promise of glory, a sweet betraying call from the mouth of the eternal Judas. The dark-birds led it, and it followed them.

In a moment, in that greater blaze, the star was lost to view.

Karlovic's breath came out of him in a long sigh. The only way it could be destroyed. Even its appetite for thermal energy could not swallow a sun.

"The darkbirds are coming back," Durham said. Then, wonderingly, "But they're not—"

The darkbirds were coming back from the green sun toward Jubb's ship. And not toward any planet. They were flying like blurring shadows toward outer space, and if they heard Jubb's calling voice they paid no heed at all.

"They're gone," Karlovic said unbelievingly.

"Yes," said Jubb, very slowly. "They obeyed that order, but it was the last." He looked at the humans facing him, the men of Earth and the men-of Nanta Dik. He said, "Do you see now that there is no difference between us, that we of Senya Dik can teach betrayal just like men?"

Durham looked out into the shining void but there was no sign now of the fleet and flying shadows. Intelligences, minds, beyond the understanding of heavy creatures like himself and Jubb. He wondered how far they would go, how long they would live, what things they would see.

Darkbirds, darkbirds, will you come back some day when we of flesh are ghosts and shadows, to frolic on our lonely worlds?